All of the illustrations in this book (except for the endpapers)
are from the series *The Night Before Christmas*, which Grandma Moses
painted in 1960. The endpaper illustration, *Out for Christmas Trees*,
was painted in 1946.

FRONT COVER: Detail from *Santa Claus Is Here*
BACK COVER: Detail from sketches for *The Night Before Christmas*
TITLE PAGE: Detail from sketches for *The Night Before Christmas*

" 'Twas the night before Christmas...": *The Night Before Christmas*
"The children were nestled...": *Waiting for Santa Claus*
"When out on the lawn...": *Christmas Garden*
"When what to my wondering eyes...": *Santa Claus Is Here*
"More rapid than eagles...": *Here Comes Santa Claus*
"To the top of the porch...": *So Long Till Next Year*
"So up to the housetop...": *Santa Claus No. 4*
"As I drew in my head...": *Down the Chimney He Goes*
"His eyes, how they twinkled...": *You Better Be Good*
"He was chubby and plump...": *Jolly Old Santa*
"And laying his finger...": *Santa Claus No. 3*
"But I heard him exclaim...": *Santa Claus No. 1*

Grandma Moses illustrations and compilation copyright © 1991
Grandma Moses Properties Co., New York. All rights reserved
under International and Pan-American Copyright Conventions.
Published in the United States by Random House, Inc., New York,
and simultaneously in Canada by Random House of Canada Limited, Toronto.

Photography by Jim Strong

*Library of Congress Cataloging-in-Publication Data*
Moore, Clement Clarke, 1779–1863. [Night before Christmas]
The Grandma Moses Night before Christmas / by Clement C. Moore.
p.   cm. Summary: Paintings by Grandma Moses illustrate
the well-known poem about an important Christmas visitor.
ISBN 0-679-81526-0 (trade) — ISBN 0-679-91526-5 (lib. bdg.)
1. Santa Claus—Juvenile poetry. 2. Christmas—Juvenile poetry.
3. Children's poetry, American. [1. Santa Claus—Poetry.
2. Christmas—Poetry. 3. Narrative poetry. 4. American poetry.]
I. Moses, Grandma, 1860–1961, ill.   II. Title.   III. Title: Night before Christmas.
PS2429.M5N5   1991b 811'.2—dc20   90-24145

Manufactured in the United States of America   10 9 8 7 6 5 4 3 2 1

# The GRANDMA MOSES Night Before Christmas

POEM BY
CLEMENT C. MOORE

Random House 🏠 New York

'Twas the night before Christmas,
    when all through the house
Not a creature was stirring,
    not even a mouse;

The stockings were hung
    by the chimney with care,
In hopes that St. Nicholas
    soon would be there;

The children were nestled
all snug in their beds,
While visions of sugarplums
danced in their heads;

And Mamma in her kerchief,
and I in my cap,
Had just settled down
for a long winter's nap.

When out on the lawn
  there arose such a clatter,
I sprang from my bed
  to see what was the matter.

Away to the window
  I flew like a flash,
Tore open the shutters
  and threw up the sash.

The moon on the breast
  of the new-fallen snow
Gave a luster of midday
  to objects below,

When what to my wondering
   eyes should appear,
But a miniature sleigh
   and eight tiny reindeer,
With a little old driver,
   so lively and quick,
I knew in a moment
   it must be St. Nick.

More rapid than eagles
    his coursers they came,
And he whistled, and shouted,
    and called them by name:

"Now, Dasher! now, Dancer!
    now, Prancer and Vixen!
On, Comet! on, Cupid!
    on, Donner and Blitzen!

To the top of the porch!
    to the top of the wall!
Now dash away! dash away!
    dash away all!''

As dry leaves that before
    the wild hurricane fly,
When they meet with an obstacle,
    mount to the sky,

So up to the housetop
  the coursers they flew,
With a sleigh full of toys,
  and St. Nicholas, too.

And then, in a twinkling,
  I heard on the roof
The prancing and pawing
  of each little hoof.

As I drew in my head
  and was turning around,
Down the chimney St. Nicholas
  came with a bound.

He was dressed all in fur,
  from his head to his foot,
And his clothes were all tarnished
  with ashes and soot;

A bundle of toys
  he had flung on his back,
And he looked like a peddler
  just opening his pack.

His eyes, how they twinkled!
    his dimples, how merry!
His cheeks were like roses,
    his nose like a cherry!

His droll little mouth
    was drawn up like a bow,
And the beard on his chin
    was as white as the snow;

The stump of a pipe
    he held tight in his teeth,
And the smoke, it encircled
    his head like a wreath.

He had a broad face
    and a round little belly
That shook when he laughed
    like a bowl full of jelly.

He was chubby and plump,
    a right jolly old elf,
And I laughed when I saw him,
    in spite of myself;

A wink of his eye
    and a twist of his head
Soon gave me to know
    I had nothing to dread.

He spoke not a word,
    but went straight to his work,
And filled all the stockings;
    then turned with a jerk,

And laying his finger
    aside of his nose,
And giving a nod,
    up the chimney he rose.

He sprang to his sleigh,
    to his team gave a whistle,
And away they all flew
    like the down of a thistle.

But I heard him exclaim,

    ere he drove out of sight,

"Happy Christmas to all,

    and to all a good night!"